UNDERCOVER OPERATIONS

UNDERCOVER OPERATIONS

A Manual for the Private Investigator

KINGDON PETER ANDERSON

A CITADEL PRESS BOOK
Published by Carol Publishing Group

First Carol Publishing Group Edition 1990

Copyright © 1988 by Kingdon Peter Anderson

A Citadel Press Book
Published by Carol Publishing Group

Editorial Offices
600 Madison Avenue
New York, NY 10022

Sales & Distribution Offices
120 Enterprise Avenue
Secaucus, NJ 07094

In Canada: Musson Book Company
A division of General Publishing Co. Limited
Don Mills, Ontario

First published in 1988 by Paladin Press

Manufactured in the United States of America
ISBN 0-8065-1166-4

10   9   8   7   6   5   4   3   2   1

Contents

■ ■ ■

Introduction

■ ■ ■

Mission Statement

The role of the private investigator in the commercial or industrial setting is multiple and complex. Unlike the sworn police officer, the private investigator's primary obligation is to his client. Though licensed by the state in which he operates or resides, the private investigator has no enforcement obligation concerning the law; he is required to obey and uphold the law to the same extent as any citizen, and his investigations and operations must not violate the pertinent statutes governing private detectives and protective agents. However, any act of law enforcement by the private investigator is done at the discretion of the client he is working for, and usually coordinated with the appropriate police agency.

During the course of a given investigation, the private investigator may well uncover client employees in violation of the law, as well as in violation of the client's company policies and regulations governing their employment. In such a situation, the private investigator must submit complete reports to the client, and allow the client to make any and all decisions relating to the dispensation of the case or potential prosecution for unlawful activities uncovered during the course of the investigation.

If the client determines that criminal prosecution is in order, the investigator then acts as a knowledgeable witness as the client may direct, although many commercial clients often choose to keep the role the private investigator has played entirely confidential. Should the client decide to exercise that option, the private investigator must abide by the client's wishes. Statutes governing the operations of private detectives in most states usually require investigators to keep all aspects of investigations confidential, and report their findings only to their clients or to corporate officers and representatives designated by the clients.

Throughout history, private investigators have been scorned by conventional law-enforcement agencies and officials. However, that is beginning to change. In a 1985 training seminar for police officers from northern Minnesota, John X. Paquette of the Minnesota Bureau of Criminal Apprehension stated that more and more police agencies and officers were cooperating with private investigators in modern times, especially concerning cases involving insurance fraud and arson. Paquette stated that patrolmen and even command officers in smaller police agencies often lack the expertise to handle such specialized investigations, and improper handling can result in the loss of an important conviction.[1]

There is no doubt that private investigators specializing in insurance fraud, arson, undercover operations, and related fields do indeed have more expertise in the handling of such cases than the average policeman, who tends to be a "jack-of-all-trades." Although such respect from the law-enforcement community is a welcome relief, the private investigator's primary obligation remains his clients' best interests and complete satisfaction, whatever that may entail.

[1]John X. Paquette, "Investigation of Property Crimes Course" (Course presented by the Minnesota Department of Public Safety, Police Training Section, Brainerd, Minnesota, 3-4 December 1985).

The private investigator is not in competition with the police. Rather, he is a businessman in the business of investigation for paying clients, a detective *for hire*. A client's reason for retaining the services of a private investigator may be that he has not been satisfied with the efforts of conventional law-enforcement agencies, or that he does not agree with their findings. Other reasons may be that the client's problem is simply a civil or personal matter that is not the concern of the police. In situations such as "honesty testing" for retail clients, or undercover operations, the client may have no immediately discernible problem, but may wish to conduct the investigation as a preventative measure to determine whether or not any problems do exist, and to ensure that small problems do not mushroom into larger ones.

There may also be insurance considerations; a corporation that has recently suffered a loss and filed an insurance claim may be required to take steps toward improving its company's security or risk losing its insurance. An investigator may also be called in to support a client company's insurance claim that is being challenged by the carrier.

There are many fields of investigation in which a private detective may choose to specialize. Undercover operations, which are also called "internal surveys" or "internal audits," offer what can be considered the most unique and perhaps intriguing field. It is this field that we are primarily concerned with here, and this manual is intended to serve as a guide for the novice investigator. This manual's purpose is to familiarize the novice with the theories and techniques involved in undercover operations, problems which are likely to be encountered, and the overall structure of such an investigation. No two cases are the same, and the private investigator's best tool is his own initiative. However, the proper training and the appropriate professional and academic background are essential for one wishing to become a successful private investigator.

Chapter 1

■ ■ ■

Preparation for a Career in Private Investigation

Professional investigators seldom agree on what kind of background a prospective candidate should have for an investigative position. Most investigators who hire employees to work in the field usually desire a background that is at least somewhat similar to their own. Some resent prospective employees who are better educated than they are, and there is a strong tendency to discriminate against youth. There are few large detective agencies that employ a significant number of investigators; Pinkerton's, Inc., is virtually the only one. Most detective agencies are small, one- or two-man operations, and many are larger than that but strictly local operations. It is financially desirable to obtain one's own license and go into business for one's self, but most states require each license applicant to submit documented proof of substantial experience in the field, such as having worked for a licensed agency for a minimum of three years, or having been employed as a police officer or federal agent for a similar amount of time. Applicants must be of legal age, and have no criminal record, though there are exceptions to the latter. Other licensing requirements may include bonding and liability insurance, and there is often a residency requirement; applicants must be residents of the state for at least six months to a year. Some states also require a written examination based largely on state laws and criminal procedures.

An individual license can cost anywhere from $100 to $500, while a corporate business license for an actual detective agency can run as high as $850. The given state's statutes govern the licensing procedures, and applications are handled by the state's Department of Public Safety, crime bureau, etc., and are often administered by a state board. The initial licensing process can take as long as ninety days to accomplish.

License applicants must meet the state's requirements, but employees the applicant later hires need not have any experience, though a background investigation is often required in that the prospective employee must have no felony record. A license holder may recruit "rookies" and train them himself.

Most small detective agency license holders tend to be retired police officers or federal agents, and few have spent their entire careers as private investigators. Such men tend not to hire youthful investigators, and often do not believe a young man who has not spent years in law enforcement "on the street" could be effective as an investigator. Larger firms, such as Pinkerton's, tend to hire young and inexperienced personnel due to the strenuous demands of the undercover work they must perform and the relatively low compensation. Also, the undercover operations as performed by Pinkerton's "Special Investigators" must by their very nature involve entry-level positions in a client's company, positions generally occupied by younger men. Many of the clients' crime-related problems involve violations traditionally committed by younger employees as well, such as petty theft, drug abuse, and vandalism to company property.

There can be little doubt that undercover investigation is a young man's profession. The stress involved in such work is unparalleled in any other profession, and the hours involved are not exactly conducive to a successful family or personal life.

According to the National Institute of Justice, the highest levels of employee theft from the workplace are committed by unmarried males between the ages of sixteen and the mid-twenties.[2] The employees who fall into this general category also tend to be more inclined toward narcotics and alcohol abuse and overall nonproductive behavior. Of course, such offenses are not exclusive to these employees, but the significant majority of offenders do fall into this category. Consequently, it naturally follows that the investigator, whose objective is to penetrate the workplace and determine the level of criminal activity there, must "fit in" as well as he can. In order to accomplish this, the investigator must have as much in common with the violators as possible, especially if he is to gain their confidence and cultivate information.

A competent investigator in the undercover field uses pretext and deception as his stock-in-trade. However, some things simply cannot be falsified. For instance, it is generally not possible to lie about one's age, except to a minor degree, and race is virtually impossible to alter or conceal. These two factors are very important considerations in dealing with undercover operations, as an investigator who does not share these things in common with the subjects of his investigation will have a great deal of difficulty in gaining their confidence.

Ideally, the undercover investigator should be at least twenty-one and under forty years of age. Individuals younger than twenty-one may be ineligible for a

---

[2] U.S. Department of Justice, National Institute of Justice, *Executive Summary: Theft by Employees in Work Organizations,* prepared by John P. Clark and Richard C. Hollinger (Washington D.C., September 1983), 29-36.

license, and may face credibility problems with clients as well as the subjects of an undercover investigation. Clients may be hesitant to entrust a youthful investigator with their case, and older criminals may scorn such a person, who in their eyes is "just a kid."

Conversely, an older investigator endeavoring to conduct an undercover operation may be avoided by the younger criminal element, which generally feels that older people are too "conformist" and too likely to turn them in to the authorities or their employer. Credibility is essential when attempting to gain the suspects' confidence, and an investigator who starkly contrasts with the subjects of his investigation may not be able to gain that vital credibility.

A college degree in law enforcement or criminal justice is not an absolute necessity for a private investigator, but it is highly recommended. An understanding of the law is important given the criminal nature of many investigations, and it can also be very helpful in dealing with the police, a confrontation that is inevitable if the client chooses to prosecute offenders. Additionally, a degree in law enforcement is an important factor in establishing an investigator's professional credibility with potential clients or a detective agency the novice investigator aspires to work for.

Law-enforcement courses covering such topics as the collection and handling of evidence, criminal law, criminal investigation, and police operations are of particular value to the private investigator. Photography courses should also be taken, as a private investigator must have a good working knowledge of cameras in order to conduct surveillance operations and secure photographic evidence.

Since many prospective clients have problems involving workers' compensation, the investigator should have an excellent and complete understanding of related laws in the state in which he intends to operate.

Aside from technical and academic requirements, an investigator must have a tremendous level of stamina for handling stress. He must be able to think on his feet and be able to remain cool and calculating while under increasing pressure. In undercover work, it is obviously important to be able to lie like a "pro" and be believed. Failure to lie convincingly may cost the undercover agent his life, to say nothing of blowing the operation. It is generally advisable to borrow enough from the truth so that the undercover investigator can remember what he has told to the subjects of the investigation. Still, he cannot be so candid as to reveal too much about himself or his personal life, thereby endangering his undercover identity.

Perhaps the most important qualification for an undercover investigator is interest in this line of work. Given the danger involved, the relatively low pay (unless self-employed with one's own license and agency), and the incredibly high level of stress, one simply has got to have a particular fondness for leading a life of intrigue—the "detective bug," as it were. Intrigue is definitely a way of life.

Chapter 2

■ ■ ■

Cause and Effect

Crime in the workplace is definitely on the rise, and more and more employers are seeking the aid of private investigators to deal with such profit-draining problems as employee theft, drug abuse on company premises, industrial sabotage, vandalism, and other counterproductive behavior. It is estimated that employee theft is costing American business and industry five to ten billion dollars in losses each year, with little sign of improvement.[3] As the overall crime rate continues to rise, conventional law-enforcement agencies simply lack the resources and manpower to adequately respond to the problems of the workplace.

A study performed by the National Institute of Justice revealed that over one-third of employees surveyed in a sample from retail, manufacturing, and service organizations reported stealing the property of their employers. Nearly two-thirds also reported the abuse of sick leave, drug or alcohol abuse on the job, and the falsification of time cards. In accordance with this author's personal experience in the field of undercover investigation of such offenses, this study further revealed that the most significant cause for such mis-

---

[3] U.S. Department of Justice statistics (Washington D.C., 1983).

conduct was the employees' dissatisfaction with their employment and working conditions, especially supervision. The study indicates that neglect on the part of the company officers has largely contributed to this problem, and that company policy rather than sophisticated security measures can be the greatest deterrent to employee misconduct.[4] Sealing profit drains of this type must be made an organizational priority. Corporate policy should clearly define which actions are considered intolerable, and ensure that the message gets through to management and employees.

When misconduct occurs, employees must be sanctioned in an even-handed manner, regardless of their standing and position in the company.

Other findings related to this study revealed that employees involved in one form of nonproductive behavior were quite likely to be involved in other forms as well. For instance, an employee involved in drug abuse while at work was also likely to be stealing from his employer, and his overall job performance was likely to be poor. Employees who were generally satisfied with their jobs were found to be far less likely to engage in misconduct or criminal behavior. Consequently, those employees who feel exploited or cheated by their employers are the most likely to engage in various forms of misconduct. Such employees, feeling slighted by their employers, rationalize their offenses and feel justified in striking out at unpopular supervisors, who represent the company in their eyes, by committing acts of theft, vandalism, and sabotage, among other things.

Offenders tend to be younger due to the fact that they have less time invested in their jobs and less at stake than their older counterparts. Traditionally, com-

---

[4] *Executive Summary: Theft by Employees in Work Organizations,* Clark and Hollinger, 29-36.

panies tend to reserve most fringe benefits for senior employees, thereby leaving more youthful workers feeling slighted and left out. Also, younger workers are less likely to value their jobs because of the flexibility of their personal lives; older workers have family responsibilities, owe mortgage and car payments, and rely more heavily on job stability for a stable income. Younger workers have less to risk in terms of wages, status, career, pension, seniority, etc., and they are not nearly as threatened by the prospect of losing their jobs as their seniors would be. Since criminal prosecution is seldom used by companies to sanction apprehended thieves, the most common penalty being simply termination, the loss of a job is viewed as just a minor and temporary inconvenience to youthful offenders, and the risk is not seen as being significant to them.[5]

An article entitled "Battling the Enemy Within" appeared in *Time* magazine as the cover story for the 17 March 1986 issue. The article dealt with drug abuse in the workplace, the disastrous effects this problem has on job performance and productivity, and the efforts by companies to combat the problem.

The article revealed that concern for this problem is greatest in the industries where accidents can cost lives. For instance, since 1975, about fifty train accidents have been attributed to drug or alcohol abuse by railroad employees. Those accidents cost the lives of thirty-seven people, and eighty were injured. More than $34 million in property was destroyed.

More specifically, a Conrail employee was "high" on marijuana while at the controls of a locomotive when he missed a stop signal and crashed into the rear of another train at Royersford, PA. The accident killed two

[5] "Battling the Enemy Within: Companies Fight to Drive Illegal Drugs Out of the Workplace," *Time*, 17 March 1986, 52-61.

people and resulted in property damages amounting to $467.5 million.

The National Transportation Safety Board attributed a fatal 1983 air accident to drug abuse. Two crewmen died when a cargo flight crashed while attempting to land at Newark Airport. Autopsies revealed that the pilot had been smoking marijuana, perhaps while flying the plane. In an accident in March 1985, a New York-based air-traffic controller, who had been injecting three grams of cocaine daily while at work, put a DC-10 jumbo jet on a collision course with a private plane. At the last minute, the smaller craft was able to make an emergency landing.

Drug-abuse problems were cited in such diverse workplaces as General Motors, Southern California Edison Company, and Rockwell. According to the Research Triangle Institute, a respected North Carolina business-sponsored research organization, drug abuse cost the U.S. economy $60 billion in 1983, or nearly 30 percent more than the $47 billion estimated for 1980.

Dr. Michael Walsh, Chief of Clinical and Behavioral Pharmacology at the National Institute on Drug Abuse, notes that the number of corporations that ask him for advice on how to eliminate drug abuse in the workplace has dramatically increased.

Defense-industry officials fear that defense-plant workers who abuse drugs may become security risks. They are afraid that addicts on the payroll might sell defense secrets and technology to the agents of hostile foreign powers in order to support their drug habits. Moreover, because criminal narcotics possession charges could lead to the loss of security clearances required for many jobs in the defense industry, drug abusers are vulnerable to blackmail. These concerns are in addition to the fact that "stoned" workers may do substandard work on planes, missiles, and munitions.

There exists no accurate measure of how pervasive drug abuse on the job really is, but government experts estimate that between 10 percent and 23 percent of all American workers use dangerous drugs on the job. Other research indicates that people who take drugs regularly, some 25 percent of the population, according to government calculations, are likely to use them at work or at least be on a "high" when they go to work. In a 1985 study conducted by the 1-800-COCAINE counselors, 57 percent of those calling the hotline reported that they sometimes took cocaine while on the job, and 69 percent said they regularly worked under the influence of cocaine. One-fourth of them stated that they used cocaine at work every single day.

Cocaine is overtaking marijuana as the nation's drug of choice. Cocaine is being used more frequently in the workplace partly because the intense high the drug generates often gives users the false feeling that they can perform their jobs better and faster. Moreover, cocaine is easier to conceal. It is generally snorted, rather than smoked as marijuana is, and does not give off a revealing odor like marijuana. Drug abuse, especially the use of cocaine, is increasing among executive-level employees, and is by no means restricted to laborers. Nor is cocaine simply a "yuppie" vice. Drugs are often used by blue-collar workers to relieve the boredom of menial jobs, such as production and assembly work.

Clearly, narcotics are readily available in the workplace, and dealers in offices and plants throughout the nation are contributing to the problem of drug abuse on the job. Some companies have reported drug "couriers" who even deliver narcotics directly to an employee right at his or her desk, or at his or her work station on an assembly line.

General Motors is an example of a corporation that

has used undercover private investigators to interdict the narcotics trade and related abuse within its plants. GM has used private undercover agents supervised by police to make some 200 arrests at its plants within the past several years. In the sting operation at the Wentzville plant, the company was able to hire two young former narcotics agents who unobtrusively infiltrated the plant posing as newly hired assembly-line workers when the company added a second shift. They adapted themselves to the working environment at the plant and mingled with the conventional workers. They were able to buy everything from cocaine to LSD from drug pushers within the plant during the six-month operation.

Because drug abuse spawns theft, agencies that specialize in the investigation of employee theft are increasingly in demand. The demand for the services of private investigators schooled in this type of investigation is increasing even as the problems of employee theft and drug abuse increase. Conventional law-enforcement agencies are powerless to effectively handle the incredible volume of offenses. They simply do not have the manpower to field enough undercover agents to penetrate the entire work force. Companies are also starting to realize that they cannot expect a supervisor or a standard security guard to be able to handle people involved with drugs. Consequently, a corporation that desires to actively and aggressively curtail such abuses within its facilities must turn to private investigators.

The investigative services offered in the private sector are tailored to the company's individual and specialized needs. Also, corporate officers are weary of traditional police apathy, and resent the fact that the police must handle countless cases at once, in addition to conducting regular police work. Private investigators are able to devote their undivided attention to their corporate clients, and they are far more accessible and responsive. Although the client must, of course, pay for the service of private investigation, this is usually a highly cost-effective means to eliminate profit drains and losses that would otherwise be left unremedied.

Chapter 3

■ ■ ■

Setting Up the Undercover Operation

Different agencies refer to undercover operations by different terms. Pinkerton's, Inc., refers to such cases as "internal surveys." Other agencies call them "internal audits" or "plant surveys." As a general rule, these terms refer to the activities of a private investigator, i.e., a professional investigator who does not work for or represent a conventional police agency or any other government agency or bureau, who has contracted with a commercial or industrial corporation to infiltrate the client company's regular work force under an assumed cover identity, and whose sole objective is to detect and report criminal activity and misconduct that is counterproductive to the company's standard operations.

In a larger agency, the undercover agent may meet with a supervisor to be assigned to a specific case or operation. An investigator with his own license will be responsible for securing his own business and developing his own cases, and will meet directly with the client. In either case, the first order of business is to determine the client's alleged problem and evaluate the case. Generally, it is preferable for the undercover agent to meet with the client himself to prevent any potential breakdown in communication. Such meetings should take place well away from the client's place of business so that the client's regular employees do not see the undercover agent with the client, whom they will be

likely to recognize. This could have a deleterious effect
on the agent's cover, and every precaution should be
taken to preserve the assumed cover identity from the
very outset of the operation.

During the initial client meeting, a contract for the
investigative services must be signed before any further
action is taken. The contract should spell out all of the
agreed-upon terms of the operation to protect the investigator and the agency and prevent any future mis-
understanding or liability. This is assuming the client
has made a positive commitment to go ahead with the
operation, and the investigator has agreed to handle the
case.

Secondly, the investigator must have a complete
understanding of what the client perceives to be his
problem, as well as what the client expects to accomplish by contracting for the investigation. It is important to note that the client's wishes concerning his case
must be honored at all times throughout the course of
the operation, and the investigator should take care to
hear him out before taking on the case or proceeding
with any investigation. The investigator should avoid
making snap judgments, and never form strong opinions
concerning the case based entirely upon what the client
has told him. The client is wrong more often than not
when it comes to naming likely suspects, and it should
be remembered that the investigator is not a "witch
hunter"; investigation must be based solely on facts and
evidence, and not on personal grudges or the client's
personal opinions concerning a given employee. The
investigator should make a note of the suspected
employees, but the client's suspicions may well be un-
founded, and the list of suspects is only a place to start,
not conclusive evidence.

The client should be asked to provide any documenta-
tion related to any losses his company has suffered,

especially losses that cannot be reasonably explained. The client should also provide a list of suspect employees and any workers who have access to the areas where the losses originated. If possible, the client should provide the investigator with a complete roster of all company employees, with their individual work stations and positions noted on the list. This roster will aid the investigator in identifying the employees once the operation is in progress, which is not always an easy task to accomplish.

All aspects of the client's business problems should be discussed, and the client should be encouraged to consider all of the available options and possibilities, such as whether or not offenders will be prosecuted. Most corporate clients prefer to terminate the offending employees, as opposed to prosecuting them. They generally seek to avoid any adverse publicity or scandal, and prefer to keep the entire investigation secret. This secrecy is well advised, as other employees—even honest ones—tend to resent the fact that their employer has placed an undercover "spy" into their midst. Criminal trials also draw media attention, and most business owners and managers would prefer to maintain an untarnished public image.

However, even if the client expresses no interest in prosecution, the investigator should pursue his case as if it were being prepared for the courtroom, as the client may change his mind. More importantly, complicated operations may end up leading beyond the employer's place of business, especially narcotics cases, and the client may not have the final say once the police become involved.

The client's priorities must be established as to the specific focus of the investigation. Some clients are concerned primarily with theft, and they may care nothing about drug abuse, or vice versa. Once inside, the investigator may discover numerous kinds of misconduct, and he should report every transgression to the client, but his concentration should target the client's primary complaint. It is obviously undesirable to pursue a course of investigation that is of no interest to the client and which may try his patience and waste the investigator's time.

Every case is different, but the investigator should establish a time frame delineating precisely when the investigation is to commence, and at least a tentative termination date so the investigator can gauge his actions and know roughly how much time he has to accomplish the client's objectives. A client may allow the investigation to continue as long as he feels he is being provided with useful information, though budgetary considerations place obvious constraints upon him. The minimum amount of time an operation like this should be contracted for is thirty days, and the average duration is six weeks to three months, though some cases may last much longer. It is desirable for the investigation to continue as long as it is developing successful leads; unfortunately, most clients are unwilling or unable to fund an indefinite operation. They usually have a set time limit in their mind's eye based on an arbitrary amount of time or the company's budgetary limitations.

Before going into the client's place of business to begin the actual operation, the investigator should have a clear idea as to the nature of the business, what the business sells or manufactures, and the exact nature of the suspected losses.

Once the client has delineated the problem, a cover identity for the investigator must be devised with the aid of the client. The investigator should be placed as closely as possible to the targeted problem area. However, the assumed cover must be believable, and the cover job assigned to the investigator must be one that allows for maximized personal contact with fellow employees, yet is unobtrusive and routine. The cover position should not be one that is coveted by other workers, as this may cause resentment toward the undercover agent and hinder the investigation. An entry-level position is ideal and, whenever possible, the investigator should slip into the company along with several other legitimate hirees to minimize the amount of attention and scrutiny new employees always draw.

The undercover man who infiltrates the work force should always be hired through the company's standard personnel channels, or at least maintain that appearance for the benefit of the other workers. Any hint of "special treatment" must be avoided. The newly assigned undercover man should do nothing that might arouse suspicion or animosity among the rest of the labor force. He should be neither the best employee, nor the worst, but simply average. He must become so gray that the other employees take him for granted as part of the scenery.

The investigator assuming an undercover position must use his own name and social security number for tax purposes, as he will actually be working his cover position. He will be paid accordingly, just as all other employees are paid, and the appropriate taxes reported and deducted from his check. Consequently, the information he provides to the company personnel officer and payroll clerk must be correct. However, the investigator must, of course, falsify his own background well enough to appear "legit" to the other company employees and perform a successful undercover mission. He does not reveal his own background in law enforcement and security for obvious reasons, and he must appear to be a qualified candidate for the cover position he has assumed.

The undercover agent's true nature should be known to as few individuals within the company as possible, preferably only the client and top corporate officers he may choose to inform due to their specific responsibilities and span of control. It is often necessary to inform the personnel director in order to create a cover position for the investigator that might otherwise not exist within the company, or to get the investigator hired in lieu of other, more obviously qualified candidates for an existing opening.

With the exception of the mandatory information mentioned above, the information on the undercover agent's employment application should be false, with certain exceptions. For instance, it may be necessary to pass an actual interview with a personnel secretary who is not aware of the investigator's true nature. Obviously, it would be hazardous to the operation if the personnel officer were to check with the undercover man's listed references! In most cases the application serves only as a "dummy" prop to use for the benefit of any onlookers as the investigator begins to assume his cover position. However, if an interview must be conducted with a personnel secretary or other low-level supervisors, the investigator must be prepared, and special arrangements may have to be made to set up special "references" to secure his cover. This is yet another subject which must be discussed with the client prior to the initiation of the undercover operation.

The investigator should know in advance what the cover job will entail so that he can imply that he is qualified for the job and perform it in a convincing manner. He must be fully aware of what will be expected of him from supervisors who will not be aware of his true purpose, and he must know in advance what the appropriate attire and equipment are for the position. He must also have a good, solid cover story to convince other workers that he was hired legitimately, especially if he was the only one hired at a time when there were no actual job openings in the company.

The undercover investigator must join the union if other client employees working in the same job classification as the investigator's cover position belong to one, and he must abide by all of the appropriate regulations. Of course, the union is not apprised of the investigator's mission, but dues are paid and the undercover agent is placed on the bottom of the union's seniority roster just as any new employee would be. Usually the union dues are reimbursed by the client as justified expenses. The undercover agent should only join such work-related programs and organizations as are required to secure the cover position, and he should avoid getting involved in any employer-related insurance or credit programs.

Expenses must be discussed at the outset of the investigation, and it must be established what kind of expenses the client will allow before the expenses are actually incurred. Obviously, the client wishes to keep the cost of the investigation at a minimum, so expense limits must be negotiated before the investigation commences. Such things as tools and equipment necessary to perform the cover position are likely expenses, as are funds for the controlled purchase of narcotics or expenses incurred while "socializing" with client employees after working hours in order to secure further information.

It is customary to submit written reports on a daily basis, since information is what the client is actually paying for. Most clients desire frequent verbal and personal contact with the investigator to supplement these reports, but the primary reports are made in writing, for the record. It is desirable to mail the reports to the client's home address in order to prevent compromising the investigation by having them inadvertently fall into the wrong hands in the workplace.

Some agencies, such as Pinkerton's, instruct their investigators to write their reports in the third person, which conceals the identity of the writer and protects the agent from being compromised should the report fall into unauthorized hands. The address the reports are to be mailed to must be given to the investigator or the individual responsible for typing and mailing them, and he should also be in possession of the telephone number where the client can be reached at any hour in the event that a "hot lead" or emergency must be communicated at once and cannot wait to be mailed in a written report. The investigator should also be aware of how to contact other company officers to be notified in case of emergency should the client be unavailable.

The client and other officers who are aware of the investigation must be cautioned never to contact the undercover agent in the workplace so as not to compromise his identity. Other workers would become highly suspicious if "the boss" were seen talking to a new employee with whom he would ordinarily have no direct contact.

Once all the preliminaries have been covered, an appointment should be made for the undercover agent to "apply" for his cover job. It must be clear whether or not the interviewer is aware of the investigator's true nature and, if not, the investigator must be very well prepared and fully able to pass the interview as if he were actually applying for the job. This can be a highly stressful situation; the entire operation hinges on the investigator's ability to pass the interview, and he could face the possibility of not being hired, just as any other job applicant might. Of course the client can always "rig" the hiring process, but this is a risk that should not be taken lightly, and should be avoided if possible. Any unnecessary attention from the client could severely compromise the investigator's cover, and both the operation and his personal safety rest on the security of his cover.

During the interview, the investigator must retain his composure, express confidence in his ability to do the job, and behave as if he were interested in the cover position. In an ideal situation, the client can arrange for the investigator to be hired without deviating much from the company's normal routine and arousing undue suspicion, but there are cases where the client does not feel he can completely trust his personnel officer with the knowledge that an undercover operation is in progress. This may be because the personnel director or personnel secretary is at fault for failing to discipline or discharge employees guilty of misconduct. They may be personal friends of the suspected employees, or they may be incompetent or even corrupt themselves. If there is any doubt as to the integrity of a given client executive, it is preferable not to inform him of the operation at all if it can possibly be avoided.

Assuming that the personnel director has been apprised of the operation and has participated in the decision-making process that resulted in the hiring of an undercover agent, the agent must still make a show of applying for the job for the benefit of any employees, secretaries, or management who have not been "clued in."

Complete attention to every minute detail is vital to the success of an undercover operation of this type. There is no such thing as cutting corners in undercover work, where one's life may well be at stake. The undercover agent must constantly consider how he is being perceived by the individuals he is working with in his assumed cover. He must blend in with the work force to the furthest extent possible, being as unobtrusive as he can.

There is *no* point of an undercover operation at which the agent can relax his attention or let down his guard. He must remain as alert as a timber wolf stalking its prey, even while maintaining the outward appearance of a mediocre, or even slovenly fellow employee.

During the interviewing process, the investigator should answer only those questions which pertain directly to the cover position, regardless of whether or not the interviewer is aware of his actual purpose, and he should keep his responses as brief as possible without seeming inordinately rude or uncommunicative. He should not volunteer any information, or tell elaborate lies, unless it is actually necessary to secure the cover position. The nature of the investigation per se should never be discussed with anyone within the client's workplace under any circumstances.

The investigator should come away from the interview with complete knowledge of when and where he is to report to work for the cover position on the date of commencement, as well as what he should be wearing or bringing with him. In most cases he will have to report to a supervisor who is totally unaware of the investigation.

In each situation where the investigator must confront an individual who is not aware of his actual purpose, he must lie to a certain extent to protect the operation. He should borrow from the truth enough to be able to speak convincingly, but conceal his actual background and the nature of the investigation. For instance, it would be foolish to claim to be from a city that one has never even been to. The individual one is addressing might be familiar with the area in question, and ask questions the investigator cannot answer. He will then find himself caught in an obvious lie. It is generally advisable to lie only when absolutely necessary, and then only moderately. Outlandish lies can be difficult to back up, and they are unlikely to be believed. Weaving a tangled web of elaborate deception usually isn't necessary, and will be more likely to hinder the investigation than help it.

In the event that a pre-employment physical examination is required for the cover position, the undercover agent will generally have to take and pass it, as any other employee would. The physician's and health-care staff should not be informed of the investigator's status, and the agent should simply undergo the examination as if he were a genuine job applicant.

Chapter 4

■ ■ ■

Going in Undercover

When an undercover investigator assumes his cover, he must make every effort to be convincing in his role; this factor cannot be overemphasized. He must behave as any new employee in the client's place of business would, and he should not be overly eager. The client's problem will not be solved in a day, and patience and tenacity are the keys to a successful undercover operation of this type. The investigator should concentrate his initial efforts on becoming acclimated to the situation, and be very low key as the operation begins. The first priority is to learn the cover job so that he can perform it to a passable degree. Very little actual investigation can be accomplished right away; it usually takes about two weeks to become familiar with the job and fellow employees. The investigator should not be overly inquisitive in the early stages of the operation, and he should only ask such questions as any conventional worker would ask upon taking on a new position. Too many questions too soon could alarm the subjects of the investigation and put them on the defensive, which is obviously undesirable.

The undercover agent should be one of the first employees to arrive at the beginning of each shift, and among the last to depart at the close of business. He should cultivate relationships with the other workers both on and off the work site as much as possible. Personal contact is the best way to gather information which will prove useful to the client, and the investigator should take advantage of every opportunity for conversation with the client's employees, especially during lunch and break periods.

Assuming the client is willing to pay for the additional hours of investigation, the agent should endeavor to include himself in after-hours socializing with the employees, such as going to the neighborhood bar, or attending private parties given by the other workers. The client's employees will generally be more willing to speak candidly about their misconduct if they are relaxing in a social situation, away from their workplace and out of the earshot of their supervisors. Such situations can prove to be the most valuable time spent during an undercover operation, and provide the most useful information.

An undercover agent is not on the assignment to make lasting friendships. He must be fully able to set aside his personal feelings and moral assessments for the sake of the investigation and the client's best interests. He should be friendly and accessible to absolutely every individual he encounters on the case, since this is the only way to put the subjects at ease and get them to talk to him. Obviously, an agent cannot develop information from a subject who dislikes him and will not converse with him. As time passes and the investigator is accepted by the other workers, he should begin to emulate the general attitudes and behavior expressed and exhibited by the crew. He should criticize unpopular supervisors, even as the other employees do, and express a desire to spite these supervisors if the other employees make such comments.

The investigator working undercover must remember that the lower-level supervisors are not aware of his true purpose, and will judge his job performance as they would that of any other subordinate employee. The undercover agent can be fired by such a supervisor if the work he performs in his cover position does not meet minimum standards, so he must avoid antagonizing his supervisors as best he can. However, it is preferable for the undercover agent to be unpopular with the supervisors rather than with the employees he is trying to investigate. If the agent is viewed by coworkers as being in the boss's favor, his investigative efforts will be very difficult. Those employees who may be resentful of their employer and guilty of misconduct will be extremely hesitant to trust anyone who is looked favorably upon by "the boss."

The actions of the investigator must be specifically tailored to the climate of the workplace to which he has been assigned. This climate is usually readily apparent, and senior workers frequently tend to fill the "new guy" in on the latest company gossip.

One investigative tactic that can be highly useful in undercover operations is to make candid admissions about one's own fictitious criminal background to other employees. Such "admissions" could involve drug abuse, theft from a previous employer, acts of vandalism, or whatever may be appropriate for the situation. Criminals tend to be boastful, and such admissions from an undercover agent will often prompt the subjects of the investigation to make real admissions of their own to him. This information can then be relayed to the client.

Once again, the investigator should not make outlandish statements that will be difficult to believe. He should not claim to be an international jewel thief or the French Connection. Bogus confessions and admissions made to the subjects of the investigation should be limited to low-level drug abuse and relatively minor offenses similar to those the subjects are suspected of.

The investigator should allude to an interest in criminal ventures, and make himself available should the subjects provide him with opportunities he can exploit for evidence and information, but he should not press this tactic too strongly.

Probing of this kind should not be attempted until the operation has been under way for several weeks and the other employees have already given some tangible indication of their activities. The investigator should not exhibit knowledge of their activities that he would not rightly have were he actually just a conventional employee.

Under no circumstances should the undercover agent suggest that another employee engage in criminal behavior or misconduct! This would constitute *entrapment*. The investigator must never create or attempt to create a problem in the client's workplace where none exists. His mission is to determine the level of misconduct already taking place, report such misconduct to the client, and take such action to correct the problem as the client directs. An investigator should not become an *agent provocateur;* it is not his role to entice an otherwise innocent or honest worker into any wrongdoing.

Charges of entrapment can become a tremendous obstacle for the undercover investigator, and any possibility of entrapment must be eliminated. Although the roles are not entirely similar, public criticism of government undercover tactics does have some ramifications for the private investigator. The private agent must be mindful of current social attitudes just as any businessman must pay close attention to his market, and the legal repercussions of professional misconduct can be severe. A private investigator can face civil exposure and liability, lose his job or his employer's license, or lose his own license if he is self-employed, to say nothing of blowing his case.

The use of undercover tactics by the FBI is relatively new. Former Director J. Edgar Hoover did not approve of FBI agents involving themselves in the underworld, in part because of concern that the agents might be corrupted through association with criminals, or at least be so perceived (in the public eye). As Harvard Professor James Q. Wilson remarked, Hoover "knew that public confidence in FBI agents was the Bureau's principal investigative resource, and that confidence should not be jeopardized by having agents appear as anything other than well-groomed 'young executive' individuals with an impeccable reputation for integrity."[6]

Regardless of Hoover's viewpoint, undercover operations are very much a part of today's FBI. Former Attorney General William French Smith has declared that law enforcement "must interject its agents into the midst of corrupt transactions. It must feign the role of corrupt participant. It must go 'undercover'."

In the traditional undercover operation, an agent would masquerade as a criminal and seek to involve himself in an already existing and ongoing criminal enterprise. Increasingly, however, the FBI is relying on so-called "stings" in which the criminal activity itself is bogus. In such operations, the agents themselves establish a criminal enterprise, which is supposed to provide criminal opportunities, and thus attract those "predisposed" to engage in such opportunities.

Such operations are necessarily costly and often of relatively long duration. The increased use of the technique is seen in the FBI's own statistics. The FBI

[6] U.S. Congress, House Committee on the Judiciary, *FBI Operations: Report of the Subcommittee on Civil and Constitutional Rights of the Committee on the Judiciary House of Representatives, Together with Dissenting Views,* 98th Cong., 2d sess. (Washington D.C.: Government Printing Office, 1984), 1-3.

budget for undercover work has jumped from $1 million in 1977 to $12.5 million in 1984. Undercover operations have climbed from 53 in 1977 to over 300 in 1983.

The most widely publicized "sting" operation was, of course, Operation Abscam. The disclosure of the Abscam investigation was profoundly shocking, not only because of the public figures involved and the nature of their alleged wrongdoing, but also because of the disturbing possibility that both innocent individuals and those who, but for the government's enticements, might never have engaged in criminal activity had been swept into the investigation.

Shortly after facts relating to Abscam became known, the Subcommittee on Civil and Constitutional Rights began an intensive review of the FBI's use of the undercover technique. This review spanned over four years and twenty-one hearings, and produced an enormous amount of information. The Subcommittee heard compelling testimony from individuals who were neither involved in criminal activity nor even targets of investigations, but whose lives were nevertheless severely damaged by undercover operations. The Subcommittee also heard of individuals who were targeted for investigation but who were never prosecuted or, if prosecuted, were acquitted, who have been unable to rid themselves of the taint of the investigation. In reviewing specific undercover operations, the Subcommittee was presented with disturbing evidence that these operations develop a momentum of their own, with little, if any, meaningful review by objective observers.

Notwithstanding the foregoing, the Subcommittee believes that the undercover technique, where used judiciously, can be a valuable weapon in the law-enforcement arsenal in appropriate cases.

As stated earlier, the private investigator has no enforcement obligation as does the FBI. It is obviously not the place of the private investigator to conduct such "sting" operations as the FBI has conducted in modern times. The private investigator's role is to determine the existing and ongoing problems in the client's place of business, and report such activity to no one other than the client who has himself initiated the investigation. The investigator takes no action toward prosecution or enforcement of the law without the client's prior approval, and prosecution can only be recommended by the investigator. Should the client elect not to prosecute offenders who have committed transgressions against him or his business, no further action by the investigator is warranted.

Although he is not a public servant in the sense that an agent for the FBI is, the investigator in the private sector must be fully mindful of legal considerations related to this type of operation, some of which have been discussed in the Subcommittee's report. He must also be mindful of his standing within the community as a businessman. Negative reports to the state board that granted him his license could ultimately cost him his license or perhaps even result in criminal charges. Civil action by individuals such as a client's employees damaged by professional misconduct or entrapment by a private investigator could also be a costly result.

Clients who are business owners or upper-level managers often have a great deal of anxiety concerning the losses they have sustained due to employee theft or other misconduct committed by their subordinates. These clients tend to have an intense desire for retribution, and hire investigators to vent their frustrations and help to punish those they view as disloyal employees. The investigator must never engage in client-inspired "witch hunts," and he must carefully evaluate his client's contentions as the operation progresses.

Upper-echelon managers seldom have a clear and ac-

curate conception of how their businesses are actually
being run at the lower levels, and many of their ideas
concerning the manner in which they are suffering profit losses, and who may be responsible for such losses,
directly or indirectly, are grossly inaccurate. Regardless
of whom the client names as a suspect or rules out as a
suspect, the investigator must form his own professional
opinion during the course of the investigation and carefully evaluate the facts and evidence at hand.

Client comments, such as, "Oh, Herb wouldn't steal
from me! He's worked here over twenty years!" or,
"Little Susie wouldn't take documents from our office!
She's the sweetest little secretary we've ever had!" can
basically be disregarded by the investigator. Absolutely
no employee of the client should be ruled out or overlooked when conducting an investigation, regardless of
how innocent or honest he may appear on the surface.
At the outset of the investigation, everyone is a suspect,
without exception. Suspects must only be ruled out as
the evidence disclosed by the investigation allows.

Personal impressions of the client's employees should
not be used to judge their degree of guilt or innocence.
Just because a certain individual is repulsive or unat-
tractive and has dubious personal hygiene does not
mean that he is automatically a criminal—not even if he
has "shifty eyes." Some criminals do fit certain patterns
and fall into certain categories, but criminals also come
in all sizes, shapes and colors, and the prettiest girl in
the office could still turn out to be the guilty party.

The attitudes and motivations of the client's employees are the keys to their respective guilt or innocence.
All of the employees should be scrutinized and evaluated for their level of satisfaction with their jobs and
their work, hostility for the client or the client organization, excessive income beyond what they would nor-
mally earn on the job in the client's business (and

allowing for any legitimate secondary income), criminal history, and both mental and emotional stability.

Some experts have stated that they believe American businesses lose more to employee theft than to burglary, robbery, or shoplifting combined. This author is inclined to agree. I have worked extensively in an undercover capacity, specifically targeting employee theft, and I have also been employed as a retail "store detective" with the sole purpose of apprehending shoplifters. It has been my experience that the average shoplifter steals an item or collection of items with an average value of three dollars or less, while the average employee who steals company property from his or her employer takes items of much greater value and does so on a continuing basis.

The undercover investigator should be alert to signals which could be an indication of employee theft or embezzlement. Some of the signals are:

1. Employees who live well beyond their means, e.g., driving expensive vehicles they could not possibly afford on the income they receive from their jobs.

2. Employees in possession of large amounts of cash which cannot be reasonably explained or only vaguely accounted for in an evasive manner by the individual in question.

3. Employees who give vague, ambiguous answers to questions concerning losses or handling procedures, and seem unusually sensitive to routine questioning.

4. Business or work procedures change when a certain employee or supervisor is not present.

5. Inventory or cash shortages increasing in quantity and/or frequency.

6. Declining collections.

7. Employees who turn down transfers, promotions, or vacations without a satisfactory explanation.

8. Customers who complain about errors in their

billing statements, invoices, or other accounting paper-
work.

9. Records that are rewritten, corrected, or otherwise
altered or tampered with.

10. Employees who make excessive trips out of their
work areas other than during scheduled break periods;
employees who make trips to their vehicles during
working hours; employees who make excessive trips to
the rest rooms.

11. Employees who linger in areas of the workplace
that have little or nothing to do with their particular job
or duties, especially stock, tool, shipping and receiving
areas, and areas where cash is kept or which contain a
safe.

12. Employees who routinely linger in the workplace
after their shift or the workday has ended.

13. Employees whose friends or relatives are not employed by the client but who frequently visit them at
work.

14. Employees who express an inordinate degree of
resentment at changes in the schedule or the work
routine.

15. Employees observed rifling the trash bins after
working or business hours.

Employees often steal office supplies, tools, and prod-
ucts that are manufactured by their employers. In retail
outlets, employees make use of "short ring-up" tactics at
the cashier counter to conceal money they have stolen
from the register. Restaurant employees may also use
the short-ring method to steal from the till. Or, they
may undercharge friends and relatives coming through
the checkout line where they work as a cashier. They
may also overcharge customers and pocket the difference.

Employees stealing from their employers may re-
move company property from the premises inside their

purses or lunch boxes, or they may move items they intend to steal from the original storage location to another area, such as their personal locker, for later pick-up. Some thieves who are usually assigned to take out the garbage will conceal items they plan to steal in with the trash, and then return after business hours to retrieve the stolen items from the trash bin or dumpster.

The investigator should be alert to any tools or merchandise which appears to be out of place or unattended. Some thieves will leave such items at a "drop location" to see if anyone notices what they have done, then pick up the items when they feel they can do so unobserved.

Employees may misappropriate company property or machines for personal business, such as company cars, typewriters, computers, or photocopiers. They may also use up expendable supplies for personal business, often costing their employer far more in losses than even the misdemeanant employee realizes.

Embezzlement may be in the form of simple padding of an expense account or an elaborate scheme involving the complicated juggling of company ledgers. Nonexistent employees may be added to the company payroll, or unauthorized payments may be made to bogus suppliers.

Other forms of employee theft may involve bribery or kickback schemes. Employees may be selling trade or business secrets "under the table" to rival companies for a fee. Supervisors may overlook shoddy workmanship or short orders for a kickback. The investigator should be alert for purchasing agents who seem to favor a certain supplier, or employees who seem to be inordinately "chummy" with certain vendors or suppliers.

Shipping and receiving areas are highly vulnerable to theft, and the investigator should watch for inaccurate accounting of incoming merchandise or supplies; a receiving clerk may be listing less than is actually received and misappropriating the rest. More merchandise than is legitimately supposed to be shipped may also be going out the door.

Once assigned, the undercover agent should endeavor to learn the physical layout of the client's place of business, as well as the regular work routine of the company's personnel, so that he is better qualified to spot irregularities. He should report anything he does not completely understand to the client, and mention any apparent irregularities in order to determine whether or not the client views them as significant or unusual.

The undercover agent must keep his finger on the pulse of the employees' morale, as this has a great deal to do with any misconduct. Workers who frequently voice an inordinate degree of animosity toward their employers are likely suspects for criminal acts committed against the employers. More often than not, spite rather than greed is the primary motivation for employee theft.

The investigator working undercover should not display concern over company losses or the misconduct of his fellow employees. Rather, he should give the suspected parties the impression that he approves, or at least does not seriously object to such behavior. This is done to preserve the agent's cover, as well as to further cultivate and ensnare the perpetrators. He should try to avoid directly engaging in the acts of misconduct himself if at all possible, although some participation may be necessary to gain or retain credibility in his undercover role. For instance, the investigator should not make it easier for employees to steal, or take action that would increase their chances of success. He may have to "steal" a small item or two to demonstrate to the suspects that he, too, willingly steals from the company. He would then secretly return the item to the client and advise the latter of the necessity of performing such a ruse for the benefit of the suspects.

Under *no* circumstances should the investigator engage in narcotics abuse with other client employees unless he feels confident that he can fake it and still be convincing. Being an undercover agent is not an excuse to commit unlawful acts, even with the client's permission. Besides the legal considerations, narcotics are nothing to play with, and no case is worth jeopardizing one's own health. Drug pushers aren't known for their concern for another's well-being, and there is no telling at first glance what a given batch of cocaine, or even marijuana, may be laced with. Even the most experienced narcotics investigators must rely on laboratory analysis for that.

Above all else, nothing is more important for an undercover agent than keeping a clear head at all times, and in a potentially life-threatening situation like this, the first mistake could also be his last. Illegal drugs are illegal for a reason, and part of that reason is the manner in which they alter the mood and the mind. An investigator working undercover *must* abstain from anything that will hinder his own mental processes, even marijuana and alcohol. He must be able to think and act as quickly as the situation may demand. The effects drugs have on the mind and the body are deceptive, and tend to "creep up" on you. Even the slightest indulgence will take its toll, perhaps a higher toll than the investigator realizes until it's too late.

The agent is the one who should have the advantage, and there is no point in surrendering it to the suspects by disabling oneself with narcotics. Let them think you are stoned—slur your speech, pretend your coordination is off—but don't get stoned. The bottom line is this: *Do not take unnecessary risks.*

When the undercover agent is faced with situations involving narcotics, whether the substance is offered for sale or gratis during a social situation within the confines of the operation, he should play along to the furthest extent possible, but decline the actual use of the narcotic substance. He should offer an explanation, such as, "That stuff gives me a headache," or "I don't touch that stuff anymore—it costs too much money." Obviously, some situations call for the controlled acquisition of illegal drugs, and the investigator is deliberately trying to induce the suspects into selling him a controlled substance. In such a situation, the investigator must use his own initiative, and put forth an appropriate response that is tailored to the individual situation and the people he is dealing with. To avoid the necessity of actually using the drugs himself, he can offer to make a purchase ostensibly for his own later use, or as a "present" for a fictitious girlfriend, etc. He can also continue to "rope" the suspects, and allude to an ability to help the pushers expand their business, the implication being that the investigator will help to further distribute their "product." Of course, in actuality, the dealers' "product" will eventually be "distributed" to the court when it is entered into evidence against them, but the undercover man must put on a good show for his suspects in order to further reel them in.

Some investigators who work primarily in the field of narcotics face this situation all the time. While in conversation with known suspects, the undercover agent is offered a "joint" as it is being passed around, or the group of suspects gets together with the agent for the purpose of discussing business over a "joint" or a "bowl." The investigator can pass the joint or pipe to his lips and feign inhaling; this is the wisest course of action.

An investigator can also have a standard tobacco

cigarette going at the same time, the smoke from which will help to conceal his ruse with the marijuana or hashish, etc. A "bong" or crack pipe can be held against one's closed lips, with the lighter igniting the bowl for the visual effect; the investigator simply does not inhale, and pretends to be holding the smoke in.

Pills are even easier to fake. A pill can be secreted away for later use as evidence, and the agent can pass his hand over his mouth as if he actually took it. It is not a good idea to hide it under the tongue, as the swallowing reflex may cause the investigator to inadvertently ingest the drug, or the drug may start to dissolve in the mouth.

Extreme care should be taken in situations involving the use of intravenous needles, especially considering the ongoing AIDS epidemic. The investigator should not even risk a scratch from a needle that has been passed around in a crowd of junkies. As a general rule, the private investigator will not be likely to encounter this form of drug abuse, as he is primarily concerned with the more common forms of abuse typical of employees in a work-related setting, such as marijuana, hashish, speed, and cocaine. Very few "needle freaks" are even capable of holding down a job. As disturbing as this nation's drug problem may be to the private investigator, it is not his job to single-handedly save the world; professionally speaking, he is only concerned with his client's best interests and expressed wishes. After all, the client is funding the operation, and it involves his business. Investigation is the private detective's business; being society's avenging angel is not.

Chapter 5

■ ■ ■

The Report of Investigation

Written investigation reports are the private detective's primary work product, and virtually nothing is more important to the paying client than accurate and timely reports. The information contained in these reports is what the client is actually paying the investigator for; the client is seldom present to witness the actual investigative process firsthand, and can only make a judgment as to the quality of the work from the end result, which he can hold in his hand and read. Consequently, well-written reports should be every investigator's top priority.

The style and manner in which reports are written will depend on the agency and the clients' preferences. Some agencies, such as Pinkerton's, require their investigators to write their reports in the third person to avoid compromising the investigator's identity. The name of the undercover investigator is never used, except in the third person, as if he were simply another individual observed at the scene along with the suspects. An unknowing individual reading the report would not be able to recognize that the writer was any of the persons mentioned in the report, and only the investigator's number is given as a signature, e.g., "567 Reports." Other agencies, such as Intrepid, require that the reports be written in the expository style of a police

report, with a synopsis of the complete report at the top
of the first page. The synopsis allows command officers
to keep abreast of each investigation without having to
read every jot and tittle contained in each report.

In any case, the most important things are that the
reports be legible, complete, timely, and accurate. They
must give the client a comprehensive overview of the
period of investigation the report is intended to cover,
and include any and all significant details.

It must be remembered that the client was not present during the investigative process, and the report
must address a reader who may know little or nothing
of the situation the report describes. Besides, the client
is entitled to complete information; he paid for it, and it
belongs to him.

As stated above, the structure of the reports will vary
from agency to agency, but certain items should always
be covered in reports generated by an undercover operation. Some examples are as follows:

1. Training and instructions given by the client's
company supervisors when the investigator initially
assumes his cover position.

2. How the investigator was received by the client's
regular employees when the operation commenced. Reports should continue to reflect the employees' attitudes
concerning the undercover agent as the operation progresses.

3. The overall quality and efficiency of supervision
within the client's place of business.

4. The physical condition of the workplace, including
physical security, locks, alarms, safety equipment, etc.

5. The employees' overall morale, general attitudes
toward their employer and the company they work for,
and any significant complaints they may express.

6. The overall efficiency of the daily work routine
and the productivity level of the labor force. The report-

ing investigator should comment on the availability of equipment and supplies, shortages, deliberate spoilage or sabotage, and any unnecessary waste of materials.

7. Any and all safety hazards, negligence, or anything that may jeopardize the health and welfare of the employees.

8. Any and all criminal behavior, especially obvious violations of the law and company regulations such as theft, drug and alcohol abuse, vandalism, sabotage, fighting, gambling, time-card irregularities, unauthorized use of company property, falsified records, and anything else the client may be concerned about. Anything in the client's workplace that may constitute a security risk should be reported.

9. Any hazard or condition that may expose the client to civil liability, such as work-related accidents, favoritism or discrimination, sexual harassment, etc.

During the course of an undercover operation, there may well be days when virtually nothing happens that deviates from the normal work routine, and all the novice investigator may feel he has to report is that he showed up for work, performed the work, and went home. This is totally, totally unacceptable! It must be remembered that the client is *paying for investigation,* and not just the labor performed in the assumed cover. A client who is billed $20.00 an hour for the investigation of his personnel does not want to read that the agent came to work, worked, and went home.

When it comes to undercover operations, there is no such thing as a day when nothing happened! Something happens *every single day* in a plant or a business full of people. Talking to people is the method used by undercover agents to gather information, and every day the agent spends inside the client's location must count. The investigator must talk to as many people as possible, as much as he can, and the results of these conversations must be reported. Even if most of the conversations consist largely of small talk or develop no useful leads, the investigator should demonstrate that he aggressively engages the client's employees in conversation throughout the day as the work routine permits, if only to show the client that actual *investigating* is being done.

If little or no useful information is developed during a given day, the investigator should comment on the areas listed in the nine items above, and expound on general areas of interest or concern. Regardless of how uneventful a day of investigation was, the client should never be given a report that is less than two pages long. Good reports result in satisfied clients, and no client will be satisfied with a scant paragraph or two for a full day's work and a full day's pay. Any investigator worthy of the title who spends eight hours in a building full of people should be able to write a *minimum* of two pages at the end of the day.

The reports should continue to monitor employee morale, and reflect any hostile comments by workers, especially any that allude to threats to the client or any plans to commit hostile acts against the client's organization. Any employees overheard making such threats should be quoted in the reports *verbatim;* the investigator should never paraphrase them. There are no "idle threats" in an undercover operation; as the investigation progresses, the agent can appraise the situation as the evidence develops, but no threatening or hostile remarks should be ignored.

The client's employees should be identified in the reports by their full names, if known, and every effort should be made to ensure positive identification. The investigator can determine the suspects' full names from the roster provided by the client, or by closely following the suspects as they punch out if a time clock is used at the client's business; full names are usually listed on time cards. Nicknames should not be used in the investigation reports unless the individual is commonly known by a given nickname, and the report should also indicate the person's full legal name.

It must be remembered that the investigation reports could be used in court, and a nickname is not sufficient identification for legal purposes. When a nickname is used in the investigator's report, the individual's full name must be listed in brackets next to the nickname. This is especially important in situations where an individual may have a very common nickname, such as "Butch" or "Stretch."

Physical descriptions of employees and all individuals mentioned in the investigation reports must be included. It must be remembered that the client may have many employees, and may not know to whom reference is made. Physical descriptions of a suspect are also very important in court. Descriptions should include:

1. Race
2. Sex
3. Age or approximate age
4. Height or approximate height
5. Weight or approximate weight
6. Build (light, heavyset, obese, etc.)
7. Complexion (fair, medium, dark, etc.)
8. Hair color
9. Eye color
10. Facial hair
11. Any distinguishing scars, marks, or tattoos
12. Any other outstanding features, such as eyeglasses, any prosthesis, acne, walking with a limp, etc.
13. Any unique clothing item that is worn frequently, such as a baseball cap with a certain logo or a certain jacket.

The employees' jobs, duties, and work stations should also be noted in the reports to give the client a complete picture of the individuals in question.

All misconduct and criminal behavior committed by the client's employees should be described in minute detail in the report that covers that time period; since most investigation reports will be daily, the incident should be described in the report issued for the day the incident occurred. All individuals involved must be positively identified as completely as possible, with accompanying physical descriptions. The nature of the offense should be spelled out specifically and accurately, with nothing left to the imagination. Upon reading the investigator's report, the client should be able to picture the events in his mind exactly as they happened.

Significant events should not be embellished, nor should they be understated. The investigator's reports must present fact as fact, and conjecture as conjecture. Reports of this kind must never mislead the client in any way, or imply guilt where it is not supported by the evidence. There is nothing wrong with an investigator presenting his own opinions and speculation in his own reports, as long as he has made it clear to the client that the information contained therein is indeed his professional opinion, and not a proven fact, where appropriate. Throughout the course of the investigation, the agent may well feel the need to "forecast" the likely behavior of certain suspect employees and the end results of certain policies or conditions as he sees them from his unique position, undercover. However, there can be no vague or ambiguous statements in an investigation report. Everything must be clear and concise, with all information spelled out in no uncertain terms.

Truthful reports demand truthful supporting evidence, and the motives and personal interests of witnesses and informants must be evaluated by the investigator in making a determination as to whether a piece of information is fact or fancy. The investigator must "consider the source," and ensure that the client is provided with an accurate picture as to the validity of all reported information.

The client who has contracted for the services of a private detective is relying heavily on the accuracy and integrity of the investigation reports in order to determine how he should handle his company's problems. The future of the client's business is at stake, and errors in the reports could be very costly for both the client and the investigator.

Although the regular employees in the client's company will not be aware of the undercover agent's true nature, they may still have cause to lie or exaggerate to the investigator concerning their own misconduct or that of a fellow employee. For example, a given worker may lie to defend a coworker he values as a personal friend, or he may lie to malign a coworker he is not particularly fond of. The motives of the undercover agent's source of information must be painstakingly evaluated before the information is passed along to the client in the investigation report.

In some trial courts, one of the questions often asked in challenging a prospective juror is, "Do you have resting upon your mind any prejudice or bias, for or against the prisoner at the bar?" Almost invariably, the answer is no, and the lawyer must become more specific before the man questioned will know what he means. The prospective juror has a better idea of how to answer when the questions are framed as follows:

1. Do you know Mr. Doe?
2. Have you ever had any dealings with Mr. Doe?
3. Are you on friendly terms with Mr. Doe?
4. Have you ever had any trouble with Mr. Doe?
5. Did Mr. Doe pay you to come here?

6. Do you own any stocks in Mr. Doe's company?
7. Did Mr. Doe's lawyer ever represent you?[7]

Likewise, in order to evaluate prospective witnesses, the investigator usually will not learn much by asking, "Have you any motive or interest in giving this statement?" Therefore, he should frame his questions along the lines illustrated above.

As the excerpt from the Bureau of Alcohol, Tobacco, and Firearms (BATF) manual demonstrates, not all subjects of an interview will be truthful or reveal their hidden motivations. An investigator working undercover is conducting interviews all day long, though in a covert manner; his interviews are surreptitious ones, disguised as conversation. Even so, the same rules apply. These covert "interviews" must be structured so as to elicit the most truthful responses and expose any bias or prejudice on the part of the subjects.

As the investigation progresses, the agent should make helpful suggestions about how to effectively deal with the misconduct and irregularities that have surfaced as a result of his investigative efforts, and he should offer the client multiple options, weighing the pros and cons of each particular option and carefully evaluating the chances of a successful outcome.

The investigator should make a continuous effort to act as a security consultant to the client, as well as an undercover agent, and offer such helpful advice on curtailing losses as he may deem appropriate. Such advice should generally concern how the client can successfully eliminate losses that have already surfaced and any that may be likely to occur or recur in the future. Safety hazards, morale, and supervision should also be ad-

---

[7] U.S. Bureau of Alcohol, Tobacco, and Firearms, Organized Crime Investigation Training Program, *Interviews and Statements* (Washington D.C., 1976), 19-20.

dressed in this regard. The investigator should not presume to give the client technical advice on the operational aspects of his business, as the private detective is generally not qualified to do so. The investigator should stick to matters that are centered around investigation and security, unless he has observed glaring inefficiency, has worked in the client's place of business long enough, and has been trained thoroughly enough to fully comprehend its operations and routine.

Below are some examples of suggestions the investigator can make to his client that could be added to an investigation report:

1. Make employee morale a high priority. Employees should be made to feel that they have a stake in the company and that their employer is actively concerned with their satisfaction and welfare.

2. Familiarize yourself with your subordinates and express an active interest in their suggestions and participation in the company. Express appreciation for the jobs they do and all of their hard work for the company.

3. Ensure that salary rates and benefits are reasonable, fair, and competitive. Employees who feel slighted or exploited by their employer may seek to "make up the difference" by committing acts of theft or embezzlement, or they may try to strike out at the company through acts of petty vandalism.

4. Ensure that management and supervisors set good examples for the workers by completely obeying all company rules and regulations. Misconduct by supervisors may encourage like behavior from subordinates.

5. Ensure that all employees are treated fairly and equitably. Eliminate favoritism and ensure that all acts of employee misconduct are treated in a uniform and just manner.

6. Devise a clear, concise set of company rules and regulations, if none presently exist. Ensure that com-

pany policies are disseminated to all employees, supervisors, and management, and enforce these policies without hesitation.

7. When an employee has been terminated for theft, drug abuse, or any other counterproductive act, publicize this fact to the entire employee population.

8. Maintain strict and accurate control of inventory, tools, and equipment, with specific employees and supervisors designated as being responsible for any losses.

9. Restrict access to valuable materials, tools, supplies, and the company's sensitive records and documents to those employees who have a legitimate work-related need for such access.

10. Limit access to the place of business to one single entrance and exit for all employees. Assign a reliable supervisor to be present at the exit during shift changes to observe all departing employees. Reserve the right to search purses, parcels, tote bags, lunch boxes, or any other container carried out of the workplace. Reserve the right to search all employees' lockers, and do not allow privately owned locks to be attached to lockers at the workplace. Make surprise, random searches of all employees' lockers.

11. Forbid all employees to leave the workplace during working hours, except during scheduled break periods. Do not allow the crew to park their personal vehicles too close to the exit or entrance to the building.

12. Check all references listed on a prospective employee's application, and make drug testing a prerequisite for hiring.

13. Discourage security and supervisory personnel from fraternizing with subordinates or becoming inordinately familiar with them.

14. Minimize after-hours access to company records, books, and computers, as well as any other company property and the premises in general. Do not allow em-

ployees to linger in the workplace after their shifts are over or after the close of business.

15. Do not hesitate to terminate troublesome and disruptive employees. Separate groups of employees who create disturbances while together; reassign them to separate working areas if termination is not warranted.

16. Do not allow friends or relatives of employees to visit them at work, with the exception of scheduled break periods or emergency situations.

Reports must address specific problems within a given client's business location, and the recommendations are naturally tailored to suit the individual client and his type of business. In the event that the investigator does not have the answer to the client's problem himself, he should be able to find someone who does. The investigator should not hesitate to consult experts or professional reference materials in the preparation of his investigation reports. References should, of course, be identified in the reports in which they are cited.

It should never be assumed that the client is aware of irregularities within his business, even if the problems are well known to the employees. All misconduct of any kind must be reported, whether or not the client is already partially aware of the problems in question. No details should be overlooked or left out by the investigator, and should be put in writing even if he has verbally apprised the client of the situation beforehand.

Under no circumstances should the undercover agent report on lawful union activities, even if he is required to join a union as a requirement for assuming the cover position. No union business discussed by the employees can be reported, and the investigator cannot report on whether or not certain employees are for or against the union. To do so would be a gross violation of the employees' rights and is against the law.

Investigation reports should not be limited in scope

to include only negative information. If a certain employee does an exemplary job in performing his or her duties and works well within the company, the investigator should point this out to the client in his report. The employees' suggestions for improving working conditions, efficiency, and productivity should also be related to the client. No one knows a specific job better than the man who has to perform it on a daily basis. It is quite likely that employees will have ideas that will benefit the company, but no channels exist for communicating such ideas to the client, who is generally a top executive or the owner of the company. The employees in a large corporation tend to view the management as hostile and unapproachable, and the investigator's reports can serve the client well in this regard. Few business owners and managers will ignore suggestions that might increase their profit margins, and they will appreciate the investigator's having brought such things to their attention. Including positive comments and observations in the reports will also demonstrate the investigator's objectivity to the client, and show that he is not simply out to "get somebody."

The problem that the client initially brought to the investigator should be given top priority, and the reports should focus on this, but all facets of the client's operations should be covered in the investigation reports. Just because the client doesn't feel he has a drug problem in his company doesn't mean he has no drug problem. During an undercover operation, the agent is very likely to uncover many problems of which the client is totally unaware.

The opinions the employees express concerning the workplace, both good and bad, are usually of interest to the client, and should be reported on a continuing basis.

In the initial stages of the undercover operation, the investigator may have little to report other than his daily work routine, the training and reception he was given, and related matters. The client's employees may not "warm up" to him immediately, and he may observe little or no misconduct before the other workers trust him completely. This is not unusual, and should not alarm the novice investigator.

The investigator's reports should become progressively more detailed as the case develops and he becomes more and more familiar with the subjects of the investigation. Continuing trends and attitudes among the supervisors and employees should be reported throughout the course of the investigation, along with any changes in such trends that the agent has observed.

The average daily report should be structured in such a way as to give the client a clear idea of how the investigator spent his billable time during the period the report is intended to cover. It should begin with the time the investigator reported for work, and include the type of work performed in the cover position. The report should include significant events that took place, along with specific details and descriptions, positive identification and descriptions of all individuals mentioned in the report, quotes and details from relevant conversations the agent engaged in with the subjects, and any other information that may be of value or interest to the client. It should conclude with the time work was discontinued for the day.

Most clients will prefer daily written reports, though some will agree to weekly ones. If a week's work is consolidated into one weekly report, the investigator must still write it as if it were five separate daily reports. The only real difference should be the heading and conclusion formalities. Complete reports should be included for each day worked, and the same rules apply. Details cannot be "fudged" just because the reports are mailed once a week instead of daily.

The investigator should examine every possible opportunity for corruption that may exist within the client's establishment, and report his findings in detail. The client is interested in anything that may be costing him money, and the agent must pursue every rumor of potential theft or corruption.

The agent should also report any rumors of theft or drug abuse from other shifts, sections, or offices that he may discover on his own shift or in the location to which he has been assigned. Such rumors are often false or exaggerated, but some can turn into valuable leads, and they should not be ignored. Company gossip can be valuable to an undercover agent tracking down corruption from inside the company. Such leads may also induce the client to request a subsequent investigation targeting the other shifts or locations, and the investigator can enjoy continued employment beyond the initial case, as well as provide further assistance to the client.

According to Charles O'Hara's classic reference, *Fundamentals of Criminal Investigation,* the purpose of an investigative report is to achieve the following objectives:

1. *Record:* The report provides a permanent official record of the relevant information obtained in the course of the investigation.

2. *Leads:* The report provides other investigators (and the client receiving them from a private investigator) with information necessary to further advance the investigation.

3. *Prosecutive Action:* The report states facts on which designated authorities may base a criminal, corrective, or disciplinary action.[8]

---

[8]Charles E. O'Hara, *Fundamentals of Criminal Investigation* (Springfield, Illinois: Charles C. Thomas Publishing, 1977), 36.

The nature of a report of investigation is an objective statement of the investigator's findings. It is an official record of the information relevant to the investigation which the investigator submits to his client. Since a case may not go to trial until months after the completion of the investigation, it is important that there be available a complete statement of the investigative results. Loss of memory in regard to details, missing notebooks, and possible absence of the investigator are some of the dangers which can damage a prosecutor's case.

Though O'Hara is primarily discussing police investigations, the same rules apply for the private investigator working undercover, especially when dealing with criminal matters. As stated earlier, the reports must be written as if criminal and/or civil action were the ultimate goal, even if the client has indicated that this is not the case. The client may not be the only voice in the matter, and the suspects in the case may also bring legal action, or the police may enter the case. There may be complications involving the labor union, advocacy groups, the county or city attorney, the police, or a myriad of other unexpected adversaries in the case. The investigation reports may be subpoenaed by any or all of the above if the case results in litigation, prosecution, or even arbitration.

There may also be complications arising from the claims of employees terminated for misconduct (based on the investigation results) for unemployment insurance. In such a case, the client has the burden of proof to substantiate allegations of employee misconduct lest he be held liable for the discharged employees' claims. Hearings and appeals in such situations may require the personal testimony of an investigator, and will certainly require his reports. In any case, there is no margin for error in a report of investigation; everything contained in such a report must be true and accurate to protect both client and investigator. The investigator must not make allegations, especially not in writing, against any individuals unless he can substantiate them.

Chapter 6

■ ■ ■

The Collection of Evidence

There are three types of evidence: observations, testimony, and exhibits. Investigation reports are often used as evidence to support the justified termination of employees guilty of misconduct, but the importance of physical evidence cannot be overemphasized.

Obviously, the undercover agent's firsthand account of any wrongdoing can be used in court as witness testimony, but stolen property should be recovered if at all possible to support the accusation of theft. When an act of theft has been witnessed, the undercover agent should make every effort to determine where the thief has stashed the stolen property, and he should be fully aware of the nature of said property. Sometimes an investigator can arrange to purchase the property from the thief, or perhaps use a pretext to gain access to the area where the thief has stored his "booty." The client may wish to provide the investigator with "dummy" property the latter can pretend to have stolen, and the agent can ply the suspect for information and advice on how to unload it, thus gaining insight as to the suspect's methods. The agent may also gain knowledge of other suspects, and follow the chain of a theft ring to the very end.

In narcotics cases, the desirable method of collecting physical evidence is to make a controlled purchase from the employees who are involved in the narcotics trade. This is accomplished with funds provided to the investigator by the client, and law-enforcement authorities should be consulted in such an event, as they may wish to make an actual arrest at the time of the purchase, thus apprehending the suspects with the evidence in hand. The investigator should have a good working knowledge of narcotics and related street jargon, and he must be able to identify the many different drugs he is likely to encounter while he is engaged in undercover operations.

Any materials involved in employee misconduct or criminal behavior should be secured as evidence, unless the evidence is not important enough to risk blowing the investigator's cover and cannot be secured without such risk. Compromising the assumed cover should not be risked just to retrieve a relatively minor piece of evidence, but evidence should be collected at every available opportunity, especially if criminal action or litigation is anticipated.

For example, if an employee is observed removing client property and he discards the container or wrapper once he is outside the workplace, the investigator should secure the container as evidence. This may also help to identify the stolen merchandise and aid in prosecution.

Film footage can be very useful in court, but this is difficult to acquire in an undercover situation, unless it is done within the context of a related surveillance operation. Also, much of the misconduct encountered during an undercover investigation takes place indoors. However, film footage of employees leaving their workplace with property stolen from the client is difficult to refute in court; the camera doesn't lie. Clients should be encouraged to arrange the setup of related surveillance operations in conjunction with the undercover cases where significant evidence of theft or drug abuse is present.

The importance of physical evidence is relative to the client's ultimate goals concerning the final disposition of the undercover investigation. In the event that the client does wish to prosecute violators, the burden of proof concerning the guilt of the suspect falls upon the investigator, who must have substantial evidence to uphold his case in court. Even if the client declines to prosecute, evidence may be required to deny an employee who has been fired for misconduct his pension, benefits, or unemployment compensation. An employee fired for misconduct may also bring civil action against the client who fired him, and seek to vindicate himself. Additionally, union employees who have been fired may seek to be reinstated through arbitration and union-related actions. In situations such as these, physical evidence can play a vital role in supporting the investigator's findings and consequently protect the client's best interests.

This author was once assigned to handle a case in which a group of paid client employees working in a nonprofit, charitable organization's plant were heavily involved in the theft of donated goods belonging to the client organization. The case was especially repugnant, in that the donated goods were intended to support rehabilitation efforts involving the handicapped, and the thieves involved were essentially robbing disabled people who desperately needed the support of the client's charitable organization.

Having been assigned to penetrate this theft ring and identify those individuals guilty of theft, this investigator was able to positively identify several employees who were engaging in frequent and significant acts of theft observed during this six-month investigation. All of the employees involved in theft were terminated by the client, but only one was actually prosecuted. The one that was prosecuted was arrested by the police and

investigators who were assigned to a related surveillance of the plant while this investigator was inside,
undercover. The theft had been predicted by this investigator, and the men conducting the surveillance were
notified in advance, resulting in the apprehension of the
suspect with the evidence in hand. The suspect subsequently entered a plea of guilty. Unfortunately, the
client was unwilling to conduct further surveillance operations, and would not prosecute other guilty employees, though the undercover investigation continued.

This investigator strongly recommended prosecution
in every case involving employee theft, but the client
refused, preferring simple termination. Consequently,
one of the employees who had been terminated but not
prosecuted for theft, a minority member, filed charges of
discrimination against the client, alleging that he had
been fired due to racial reasons. His case was entirely
without merit, as the organization employed numerous
members of his race, only two of whom were terminated
for theft, followed by one nonminority member charged
for related offenses. This investigator was called upon to
present the case against the individual in question to a
human rights attorney, and a meeting was held involving the client, the attorney, and this investigator.

The attorney was presented with nearly six months'
worth of daily investigation reports, many of which documented acts of theft committed by the complainant he
represented. The theft charges were supported with
physical evidence, such as packages and containers recovered from the items the suspect had stolen. The
investigation reports also detailed the ongoing investigative process, which documented the fact that both
minority and nonminority members were being investi-
gated for theft, and that at least one nonminority
member, a supervisor, would soon be terminated for
theft as a direct result of the investigation.

After conducting his own investigation of the situation at the plant and reviewing the investigation reports, the attorney was satisfied that no case for discrimination existed, and the case was dropped. Were it not for the detailed reports supported by physical evidence, the result could have been dramatically different.

The value of physical evidence is determined by how useful it is in verifying that a crime has been committed, identifying the person or persons who did it, and exonerating other persons who may be under suspicion.[9]

The collection of evidence is a science in itself and far too complicated to cover in a comprehensive manner here. Forensic evidence is seldom required in undercover operations of this type, as the crimes the undercover private detective is likely to encounter generally do not require such elaborate techniques. However, no opportunity to collect supporting evidence should be overlooked, regardless of the situation. It is better to collect some evidence that may never be needed than to need evidence and lose a case for the lack of it.

Any evidence secured during an undercover operation which is to be used in support of the case should be carefully packaged and labeled as follows:

1. Place the item in a Zip-Lock plastic bag. Use a sep- arate bag for each single piece of evidence collected.

2. Label the evidence by marking the following information on a 3" x 5" index card or self-adhesive label and affix this to the plastic bag:

    a. The date and time the evidence was collected.

    b. The investigator's full name and ID number.

    c. The client's name, company, and case number.

---

[9] Richard H. Fox and Carl L. Cunningham, *Investigator's Manual: Crime Scene Search and Physical Evidence* (Washington D.C.: American Police Academy, 1974), 3.

d. The nature of the evidence and the suspect or individual from whom it was acquired.

Depending on the nature of the evidence, it should be presented to the client accompanied by the related investigation reports, or retained if it is expected to be used in court.

Certain forms of evidence, such as narcotics, should be turned over to the appropriate law-enforcement agency once the client has been informed. Perishable evidence should be well preserved and refrigerated if necessary. All evidence should be maintained in a secure area, such as a locked safe, so that the integrity of the evidence can be assured. The chain of evidence should be well documented on the package or container, with each individual signing for it as it changes hands. Failure to maintain the chain of evidence may result in the evidence being disallowed in court. The investigator must be able to testify with confidence that the evidence presented in the courtroom is the same item or items that he collected at the scene of the crime. The records must show that the evidence has been accounted for from the moment it was collected until the moment it reaches the courtroom. "Tainted" evidence is little better than no evidence at all.

Chapter 7

■ ■ ■

Drawing the Investigation to a Close

As the undercover operation draws to a close, the investigator should have a very clear idea as to the validity of the client's initial complaints, any problems related to security that do exist within the client's place of business, and which individual employees are responsible for the problems. The client must be completely satisfied that the investigation has addressed all of his major concerns.

Although it is not humanly possible to be able to completely investigate every single employee to a satisfactory degree in the limited amount of time that is usually allowed for such investigation, especially in plants that employ a large number of people, the undercover agent should be highly familiar with all employees within his reach given the limitations of his undercover position and the work station he was assigned to in his cover role. In a large organization, the undercover agent should at least be completely familiar with those individuals in his section or department, and be able to accurately forecast whether or not these individuals are predisposed to criminality or future misconduct, if he has not already proven them guilty of some tangible wrongdoing.

The investigator should protect his cover identity throughout the investigation to safeguard his best interests as well as those of his client. The client's subordinates will resent the presence of an undercover agent in their midst, even if they are guilty of no misconduct. An investigator working undercover who has "fingered" employees for misconduct should preserve his cover to the end, and even work out an arrangement with the client and the police to be "busted" along with any other employees who may be apprehended as a result of the operation, assuming the case is going to end at the time of the arrest. This will convince the other arrestees that the undercover agent is "one of them," and divert suspicion away from him.

The investigator should try to avoid revealing his actual purpose to anyone other than the client and the police, if necessary. The assumed cover should never be deliberately blown unless it is unavoidable due to the need for personal testimony in court as a result of criminal or civil action.

There is no legitimate reason for the client's subordinate supervisors or employees to ever know that such an operation ever took place, so why tell them? Generally, the clients will prefer to avoid any court action, and simply terminate the guilty parties. Personal testimony on the part of the investigator is seldom needed, and the investigation reports will usually serve the client's purposes well enough. If an investigator works in the undercover field for any length of time, the risks are great enough; there is no point in compounding them, and the more publicity he gets, the more he is at risk.

An undercover agent should never carry any type of security badge or identification on his person while in the field. He should also avoid making notes in the presence of the subjects of the investigation. If notes are required for later inclusion in the investigation reports, such as to record names or account for certain details or specific times, the investigator should duck out of sight before writing them. A rest-room stall is the best location for this purpose. The agent should never carry a notebook with him on an undercover operation, unless the cover position calls for it. If necessary, notes can be written directly on the body—under the shirt on the chest or stomach—in order to avoid observation. More detailed notes can be completed once the investigator has left the site, but they should be written down as soon as possible while the investigator still has the details clear in his mind.

Like the investigation reports, the investigator's notes may end up in court, and this is something the investigator must keep in mind. As a general rule, investigation reports will suffice for any legal purpose, but the private detective must be prepared for the possibility of having his notes subpoenaed as well. An investigator may also wish to refer to his notes while testifying, especially if the case is a complicated one with many details too numerous to remember.[10]

The investigator's notebook may be used in court by the investigator to refresh his memory while testifying. Defense counsel may under these circumstances subsequently examine the notebook. The possibility of court examination of his notebook should act as a control for the investigator in regard to the care and accuracy which are to be employed in recording notes.

Under examination by defense counsel, the investigator must be able to account for all entries in the notebook. Cryptic, vague, or illegible inscriptions tend to undermine the validity of the notes and hence militate against the credibility of the witness. One of the conditions sometimes placed on the use of notes in court is that they be original notes which were taken contem-

[10]*Fundamentals of Criminal Investigation,* O'Hara, 32-33.

poraneously with the phase of the investigation to which they pertain. For example, notes describing the crime scene should have been taken on the scene itself. Of course, exceptions may be made in regard to matters such as moving surveillances or interrogations which by their very nature require that the notes should be made at a later time.

The client should continuously be cautioned against taking any action regarding the information contained in the investigation reports while the investigator is still on site and the undercover operation is still in progress. If the client disciplines an employee based on information in the investigator's reports, it could completely shatter the agent's cover and put him in grave danger. It could also bring the investigation to a screeching halt before other problems have been dealt with effectively.

Should the subject employees confront the investigator and accuse him of being a "spy" or a "narc," the investigator should remain cool and simply deny the accusation. The agent should give the appearance of having been offended by the charge, and respond with a comment such as, "You watch too many James Bond movies, pal," or "Hey, I'm just a working stiff like you, man." He must be prepared to defend and reinforce his cover at all times, even when it does not appear to be challenged.

The investigator should "live" his cover and never let down his guard or allow himself to be lulled into a false sense of security due to the inactivity of an uneventful case. Many work organizations, especially industrial plants with labor strife, are rife with suspicion and paranoia, and any new employee is scrutinized to a high degree. The undercover agent must remember that the other employees are watching him, even as he is watching them. He should never dress or behave in a manner that does not coincide with his cover position, and avoid any indication of wealth beyond the means of a regular employee.

If at all possible, an undercover agent should avoid letting the client's employees know where he actually resides, or giving them his home telephone number. He may be compelled to provide the suspects with his home phone number if the cover role requires that he socialize with them after work, but as a general rule, an unlisted, unpublished telephone number is a must for anyone working undercover.

Precautions should be taken by the investigator to protect his own safety in the event of a compromise of his cover position. Even if the case involves only trivial offenses, the investigator must not lower his defenses or allow himself to become less than 100 percent alert. It must be remembered that many law-enforcement officers have lost their lives in the line of duty while handling seemingly minor crimes; some have even been shot down in cold blood while writing out a simple traffic ticket. There are no guarantees regarding the sanity and stability of most suspects, and even petty criminals can become extremely dangerous.

The investigator's personal vehicle should have a locking hood that can only be released from the inside, and he should acquire a locking gas cap if the vehicle is not already equipped with one. A car seems to be a favorite target of vandalism for disgruntled employees who are not quite brave enough to threaten or retaliate against a private detective face to face. Weapons intended for personal defense are not always a good idea, and the frame of a gun outlined under one's shirt is as obvious a compromise of the investigator's identity as a badge worn on the lapel.

If firearms are to be carried, they must be licensed, small enough to be completely concealed, and as unobtrusive as possible to avoid any undesirable attention from the subjects of the investigation. A small .22 or .25 automatic pistol can be well concealed in an ankle holster worn inside a boot. It must be remembered that the name of the game is deception, and a *good* undercover agent will never have to use a weapon; if he has done his homework, his suspects will never be the wiser, and will never suspect his true identity or have cause to threaten him. If the operation was a success, the investigator will be long gone by the time the suspects fully realize what has happened, if they ever do at all. Many agencies do not allow their investigators to carry guns or unauthorized weapons, unless an apprehension is planned. Some clients will also be uncomfortable with the idea of an undercover agent carrying a weapon in their place of business. Still others insist upon it.

A self-employed investigator must use his own discretion concerning self-defense, but undercover work requires subtlety, and heavy-handed tactics are largely inappropriate in this field.

The undercover agent should become as familiar with the subjects of his investigation as is realistically possible, but he must not become personally involved with any of them beyond the confines of the investigation, even if the employees of the client have been guilty of no wrongdoing and the operation has drawn to a close. Word of the investigator's actual purpose may get back to other employees still working for the client, and may embarrass the client or cause him legal difficulties. The investigator should never become romantically involved with the subjects of an investigation, even under pretext of securing information. This can make the investigator look highly contemptible on the witness stand if the case ends up in court, and his testimony could be impeached. Evidence acquired in such a manner would be valueless, anyway.

Toward the anticipated end of an undercover operation, the investigator should ensure that all of his reports and evidence are in order for any hearings or court appearances that may be forthcoming. He should also prepare a final report summarizing the entire case for the record. The final summary report consolidates all of the previously submitted daily reports into one concise work, or at least the significant details and highlights contained in earlier reports. This allows the client, the investigator, or prosecutorial authorities, if necessary, to review the case without having to examine all of the numerous daily reports the investigator has submitted throughout the course of the investigation.

The investigator should discuss his withdrawal from the operation with the client well in advance of the investigation's conclusion. The client may wish to set a final date for the termination of the case, at which point the agent simply resigns for fictitious reasons. In situations where the agent has penetrated a criminal organization, such as a drug or a theft ring, and police apprehension of the suspects is desired, the agent should be "busted" right along with the suspects in a ruse that will preserve his cover to the very end. The agent can then be spirited away by the authorities and secretly released once he is removed from the presence of the actual suspects.

It is always undesirable for an undercover agent to testify in court or any type of public forum. For one thing, court documents are usually a matter of public record, and such documents are on file at the courthouse for any citizens to review at their leisure. Such public documents could blow an investigator's future cover if they reveal his identity and the nature of his work. In some cases the investigator's testimony is crucial and cannot be avoided. However, the agent's written investigation reports, notes, and sworn statements should be offered in lieu of a personal and public appearance. A public appearance should only be made if it is absolutely necessary to achieve conviction or the successful outcome of the investigation.

If the investigator is required to make a personal appearance at a hearing or in court, he must thoroughly prepare himself by reviewing his notes and related investigation reports. He should offer his testimony in a clear and concise manner, exhibiting a high degree of professionalism and objectivity. He should answer all questions directly and completely, but avoid volunteering any additional information beyond the initial questions. The well-prepared investigator who has confidence in the validity of his investigative findings cannot be shaken by the opposition in court.

The investigator should meet with the client and his representatives to discuss the case prior to giving his testimony in order to determine the client's best interests. An investigator must never perjure himself, nor should he lie to protect his client, especially not in court under oath; being caught in a lie in court can result in destroying the investigator's credibility for the rest of his career. It is the client's responsibility, or that of his designated representatives, to answer for his own actions in court, not the investigator's. The investigator is only responsible for his own professional conduct, observations, and testimony.

Bibliography

■ ■ ■

"Battling the Enemy Within: Companies Fight to Drive Illegal Drugs Out of the Workplace." *Time*, 17 March 1986, 52-61.

Fox, Richard H. and Carl L. Cunningham. *Investigator's Manual: Crime Scene Search and Physical Evidence.* Washington D.C.: American Police Academy, 1974.

O'Hara, Charles E. *Fundamentals of Criminal Investigation.* Springfield, Illinois: Charles C. Thomas Publishing, 1977.

Paquette, John X. "Investigation of Property Crimes Course." Police Training Section, Minnesota Department of Public Safety, Bureau of Criminal Apprehension. Presented at Brainerd, Minnesota, 3-4 December, 1985.

U.S. Bureau of Alcohol, Tobacco and Firearms, Organized Crime Investigation Training Program. *Interviews and Statements.* Washington, D.C., 1976.

U.S. Congress. House. *FBI Undercover Operations: Report of the Subcommittee on Civil and Constitutional Rights of the Committee on the Judiciary House of*

77

Representatives, Together with Dissenting Views. 98th Cong., 2d sess. Washington D.C.: Government Printing Office, 1984.

U.S. Department of Justice. National Institute of Justice. *Executive Summary: Theft by Employees in Work Organizations.* Report prepared by John P. Clark and Richard C. Hollinger. Washington D.C., 1983.

U.S. Department of Justice statistics. Washington D.C., 1983.